MW01517429

Something to

Prove

www.frontiercollege.ca
This book is brought to you by
Frontier College
and our generous supporters

FRONTIER
COLLEGE

COLLÈGE
FRONTIÈRE

Ce livre vous est gracieusement
présenté par Collège Frontière
et ses généréux donateurs

www.collegefrontiere.ca

Something to
have

Banting and Best

Before the discovery of insulin, people who had diabetes would often die at a very early age. It was only about thirty years before Bobby was born that two doctors at the University of Toronto discovered a way to control diabetes. As a young man, Dr. Frederick Banting had watched a friend wither away from diabetes and die. Banting became determined to find out how to help the many people who had the disease. In the winter of 1922, he and his colleague Dr. Charles Best used their research to save the life of a young diabetic boy. It was a stunning discovery, made at an incredible pace. And it was a discovery that has helped save the lives of millions of people in less than 100 years.

that Bobby, with his grittiness and determination, not to mention his love of the game, could make it in the league. And he wouldn't let anyone take that from Bobby.

When Pat heard of the NHL's concerns, he took matters into his own hands. He took Bobby to the Mayo Clinic, a highly respected hospital in the United States.

"He took me down there . . . He just wanted to confirm to the NHL brass that I was fine to play hockey and that diabetes wasn't going to affect me," Bobby says.

Sure enough, the doctors supported Bobby. They told him and Pat that, so long as Bobby took care of his diabetes — something he had been doing for four years already — he was fine to play in the NHL. Pat wanted it in writing. And he got it.

The following season with the Bombers, Bobby had 51 goals and 86 assists. He even managed to drop his penalty minutes back to 123. In the playoffs, he amassed 25 points.

Not only was Bobby great on the ice, he was also a great leader. This was something that teams considered a great

Dr. Frederick Banting and his assistant Dr. Charles Best, pose with one of the diabetic dogs they used to help discover insulin at the University of Toronto.

addition to on-ice skills. So scouts paid the Bombers a visit. Pat squelched any fears they might have had about Bobby's "affliction" with the letter from the Mayo Clinic.

Things looked promising for Bobby. He was going to make it to the NHL.

Or was he?

4 "I'll Show 'Em"

Bobby's years of playing for the Flin Flon Bombers had got him noticed. He was one of the WCJHL's scoring leaders. He could perform on and off the ice. He seemed to have all the right stuff for the NHL.

The draft most hockey fans today are familiar with first took shape in 1969, the year of Bobby's draft. That year, in the first round, first overall, the Montreal Canadiens picked Rejean Houle, a right winger from the Montreal Junior

Canadiens. The Canadiens had the second pick as well. They picked Marc Tardif of the Montreal Junior Canadiens, a left winger.

Pick after pick was called. And finally the thirteenth pick, the final one in the first round, was called. J.P. Bordeleau went

1969 Hockey Draft

Although every hockey fan knows about the NHL Entry Draft, there wasn't always a draft like this. The first NHL Amateur Draft was held in Montreal on June 5, 1963. All amateur hockey players who had reached the age of seventeen, and who weren't already sponsored by an NHL team, were eligible. But in 1969 the draft changed to allow any junior player to be selected. In that year 84 players were chosen — more than four times the average amount of players from the first six years of the draft. In 1979, the draft was renamed the "NHL Entry Draft."

to the Chicago Black Hawks.

Bobby had been overlooked.

For many, it was a surprise. A player with 1,210 points in 1,144 games was overlooked in the first round of the draft. It seemed almost unbelievable.

It was just another sign of the ignorance that surrounded diabetes. All people knew was that it was a sickness, a "disease." How could a player with any disease play a major league sport as demanding as hockey? Who would be crazy enough to invest time and money to develop a player who might pass out on the ice? Or someone who might not show up for practice or a game because he's sick?

There was one team that was willing to take that chance, a team whose very name would come to mean grittiness.

The second round started. Dennis O'Brien went to Minnesota, Rick Kessell to Pittsburgh, Dale Hoganson to Los

Angeles. And then . . .

Bobby Clarke to the Philadelphia Flyers.

Like Bobby, the Philadelphia team was new to the NHL. They had become a team just two years before, during the NHL expansion. This was when the league grew from six teams to twelve.

Right after Philadelphia picked Bobby, Sam Pollock, manager of the previous year's Stanley Cup winners, the Montreal Canadiens, approached Philadelphia with a deal. Montreal wanted Bobby. Philadelphia turned them down. Then came Detroit. The Red Wings offered two veteran players for Bobby. But Philadelphia made it clear: Bobby was not for sale. It seemed that teams had been waiting for just one team to show interest in the diabetic player before taking a chance on him themselves. But Philly held strong.

As any young man who lived and

breathed hockey would be, Bobby was thrilled. "All I wanted was a chance to show them that I could play, and I got that chance in Philadelphia.

"I basically said, 'I'll show 'em,'" he says. And show them, he did.

5 Making His Way

If you ask Bobby today, he'll tell you that being drafted by Philadelphia was an amazing feat. At the time it happened, he wondered if he had what it took to make it in the NHL. Sure, he had seen a couple of NHL games, but actually playing in a league that was known for its toughness was a different story. Bobby had always been a quiet, yet confident, person. But he still had doubts.

When Bobby started at the Philadelphia

training camp, it began to dawn on him that maybe he *did* have what it took to play in the NHL. At the very least he knew he could go one-on-one with the players of the Quebec Aces, the Flyers farm team in the American Hockey League. A farm team is where professional sports teams keep drafted players until they feel they're ready to play professionally.

Bobby still didn't think that he would make the Flyers' final roster. He thought that he would be kept with the Aces. But he wasn't. It was obvious to the coaches that Bobby had come out to play. There was nothing fragile about this kid from Flin Flon. He was big and he was strong. He was a playmaker and a good fit with the Flyers.

Training camp was different from anything Bobby had done before. There were changes he had to make. But the changes didn't come easily.

One day, he got up late.

"I forget what time I was on the ice . . . but I didn't have time to get enough breakfast. I slept in, and I just hustled over there and got my skates on. And on the way back, I had a reaction."

His "reaction" happened in the back of a taxi with a few other players. Bobby became disoriented and weak. Luckily, his teammates got him to a hospital.

Once Bobby was at the hospital, the doctors and nurses recognized his symptoms and immediately knew his blood sugar was low. They raised his blood sugar, and Bobby headed back home. Although he didn't remember being taken to the hospital, Bobby never again missed another practice . . . or another meal.

While he was playing for the Flin Flon Bombers, he had never had anything like that happen. Were the doubters right? Was the NHL going to prove to be too rough for Bobby?

One of the Philadelphia trainers did his own investigation to get to the root of what had happened. Frank Lewis figured out that, on the morning of the episode, Bobby had eaten only a light breakfast. Skipping or cutting back on meals was hardly good for a diabetic, especially a diabetic going through rigorous training. So Lewis worked on developing a special diet that would help boost Bobby's sugar before games. This diet was one that Bobby would follow for years to come.

For Bobby to keep his energy up before a game, he would drink a bottle of cola with three spoonfuls of sugar added. Between periods, he would drink half a glass of orange juice with added sugar. After a game, he would drink a whole glass of sweetened orange juice. Lewis would carry around chocolate bars and a tube of glucose for Bobby, just to be sure. The more exercise that Bobby was getting playing hockey, the more sugar he had to consume to keep his blood sugar at a safe level.

Bobby never suffered a sugar low again.

Still, even if Bobby kept his sugar lows under control, he had to produce. As with any other player in camp, he had to try to prove that he could play with the big boys.

When the final roster was announced for the 1969–70 Philadelphia Flyers, Bobby had made the cut. It was clear that the coaches had faith in him. It was clear that they didn't think his diabetes would be a factor on the ice.

Wearing number 16, twenty-year-old Bobby made his NHL debut on October 11, 1969, against the Minnesota North Stars. Standing on the ice, the tousle-haired Bobby took in the cheering crowd around him. There was no doubt that this 178-cm (5 foot 20 inch) 90-kg (176 pound) boy from Flin Flon had made it big.

Bobby in his rookie season in a game against the Toronto Maple Leafs.

But to last in the NHL, you have to be a presence. You have to make plays. You have to contribute. This takes time. So, not surprisingly, Bobby didn't score in his first game. He didn't even get a point. But his presence was definitely felt on the ice. He wasn't afraid to get into the plays. And he was physical.

Helmets

Every NHL player today wears a helmet on the ice. But that wasn't always the case. Some believe that George Owen of the Boston Bruins was the first to wear a helmet in 1928, but no one can be sure. It wasn't until the 1970s that the NHL made a rule about helmets. Any player who signed after June 1, 1979, had to wear a helmet. Craig MacTavish of the St. Louis Blues was the last player to play in the NHL without a helmet.

It didn't take long for Bobby to notch his first point. On October 22, 1969, he got his first assist against the Toronto Maple Leafs. Then came the day that all boys who dream of playing in the NHL picture in their minds: Bobby scored his first goal. It came in his sixth NHL game, against New York Rangers goalie Ed Giacomin. And it didn't come until 16:36 of the third period.

It was to be the first of many. "It's probably the only goal I know," Bobby says now, laughing.

Despite all the successes, Bobby had another adjustment to make. He was from a small town, and life in the big city of Philadelphia was something new.

"Flin Flon, where I had lived my whole life, was ten or twelve thousand people. You knew everybody and everybody knew you, and it was very comfortable . . . I got plunked into Philadelphia, where there are millions of people," Bobby once said in an interview.

Luckily, Bobby had some help. Billy Sutherland, a Flyers teammate, gave him a hand adjusting. Billy was from Saskatchewan. He and his family welcomed Bobby at their home often.

And soon, Bobby would come to consider Philadelphia a home away from home.

6 From Rookie to Star

Bobby's first NHL season wasn't exactly spectacular. That year, Tony Esposito won the Calder Trophy for Rookie of the Year. But Bobby's first season was better than average.

He played the entire 76-game schedule and earned 46 points, with 15 goals and 31 assists. His performance even won him a place on the NHL All-Star team: a pretty big achievement for a player in his first NHL season — a pretty big achievement for a player who had been overlooked in the draft by many teams.

Bobby Clarke was just getting started.

Bobby's second season had a rough start. Because of an abscessed tooth, he started his season 9 kg (20 pounds) under-weight. In the first 31 games, he had only 5 goals and 11 assists. Things weren't looking good.

But Bobby was tough, on and off the ice. On the ice, he took the hits that came his way. And he delivered plenty, too. Off the ice, he was a quiet leader for the team, but he was known as someone who was not afraid to give his opinion.

His hard work that season paid off. In the final 47 games, Bobby tallied 30 goals and 35 assists. He finished the season with 63 points. Bobby's work ethic would become legendary in Flyers history.

That season, his play helped the Flyers capture third place in the division.

Unfortunately, they were eliminated in the first round of the playoffs by the Chicago Black Hawks. But it didn't matter. The Philadelphia team was clicking. And Bobby was part of the reason they'd seen such improvement.

By this time, Bobby had settled into a routine — a routine that seemed to be like any other hockey player's.

"I couldn't expect them [the Flyers] to change anything they were doing for me . . . In those days we had steaks and stuff for lunch. It's quite different than today. Before the game, about 5:00, I'd have a dish of ice cream . . . just to make sure my sugar was up."

The trainer left cola in his locker. If Bobby felt low, the trainer would grab a cola for him to boost his blood sugar.

What no one could foresee was that there was something bigger than the NHL season waiting for Bobby. Something that would make him — and hockey in Canada — a legend. Something that would breathe life into a game that was starting to see change.

Canada has always considered itself to be the home of hockey. Sure, there's some debate about whether hockey got started in Ireland, England, or even Russia. But no matter what, Canada has become synonymous with hockey. We consider it "our game."

So it was bothersome to Canadians back in the early 1970s that the Soviet Union was saying that it was producing better hockey players than Canada.

The Soviet Union was new to the world of hockey. But during the 1960s and 1970s, they ruled the sport. Not only had they won the gold medal at the 1964 Olympics, but they had also won seven World Championships. Were the Soviets better at hockey than the Canadians?

Many thought that it was impossible. But there had to be a way to prove it.

Alan Eagleson, executive director of the

Bobby in his Team Canada jersey just before the 1972 Summer Series. It was in this series that Bobby was propelled into hockey stardom.

NHL Players' Association, decided to arrange a tournament to show the talent of the Canadian players. Some of Canada's top NHL players would compete against the Soviets' best. Four games would be played across Canada. Another four would be played in Moscow, in the Soviet Union.

Like many hockey players at the time, Bobby was interested in the tournament. But he wasn't one of the original twenty players selected for the team. Then, one day Bobby got a phone call from Eagleson. Amazingly enough, a few players couldn't or didn't want to play in the series. Here was Bobby's opportunity.

"All I wanted to do was play hockey," he says. "I didn't care when, where or anything . . . it was special for me."

The Summit Series, as the tournament came to be called, proved to be a special event for all the players involved, and for Canada.

Back in the USSR

The Union of Soviet Socialist Republics is also known as the USSR or the Soviet Union. It formed in 1922 and broke apart in 1991. The USSR was a communist country made up of many smaller republics, the largest of which was Russia. During the Summit Series, there was a Cold War going on, based in part on the differences between communism and western democratic nations, like Canada and the United States. During the Cold War, there were hostilities between countries, but no actual fighting. This added even more tension to the hockey games of the series.

7 Summitting to the Top

In Montreal, the morning of September 2, 1972, started off hot. By noon, it was already 25°C. But it wasn't only the heat. The whole city was burning with excitement. A war was brewing: a war on ice.

For months, Canadians had looked forward to the Summit Series. It was supposed to be a "friendly match" between the Soviets and the Canadians. Most Canadians thought it would be a show of the country's hockey might. They believed the Soviets were no match for Canada's best players. For years Canada's top hockey players had chosen to play in the NHL. At that time, NHL players, as professional sports players, weren't allowed to play in tournaments like the World Championship or the Olympics. But this series was arranged especially to show how good Canada's best pro hockey players were.

The sun barely peeked through the clouds as Bobby headed to the Montreal Forum. He felt hot, but he was ready to face the Soviets. They didn't know how *real* hockey was played. He and his teammates would show them what it meant to be a hockey player in Canada. After all, hockey was in the blood of every Canadian. As it was at home in Flin Flon, hockey was a way of life.

"We weren't expecting fierce competition," Bobby says.

But things didn't go as expected.

The opening ceremonies of the series started off the tournament just as any other. The fans politely applauded for each Soviet player as he skated forward to be introduced. When Canada's team was introduced, Bobby took to the ice in front of a packed Forum, which included Prime Minister Pierre Trudeau.

Ken Dryden was starting in net. The players took their places on the ice. Phil Esposito took the faceoff. The puck was dropped to the ice.

The game was underway. The Soviets cleared the puck into the Canadian zone. Esposito went down the right wing with the puck and shot it just above the goal. The puck was kept in the Soviets' end. Frank Mahovlich played the puck behind the net, passing it to Brad Park on the right wing. Park passed it to Esposito, who was in the slot. Esposito got the puck right to

Mahovlich, who was sitting to the right of Soviet goalie Vladislav Tretiak. Mahovlich backhanded the shot, but it came back out to Esposito, who slapped at it . . . and scored!

The Forum erupted in cheers. Things were looking good for Canada. After all, they had opened up the scoring at 30 seconds into the game.

Just a few seconds later, Paul Henderson was called for a tripping penalty. The Canadians managed to kill the penalty. The Soviets had a couple of good tries, but Dryden managed to keep them out of the net.

Then, almost six minutes later, Bobby was on the ice. He took the faceoff after a break in play. The young Bobby had been placed on a line between Ron Ellis and Paul Henderson. With the hard work of all three players, this line would be one of the best of the series.

The puck was iced.

The players took their places to the left of the Soviet goalie. The puck was dropped, and Bobby got it to Ellis, who passed it to Henderson, who took what looked to be a harmless shot on goal. But the puck flew to Tretiak's right and hit the back of the net. Canada had two goals!

The Canadian players were pleased to be ahead two goals in just under seven minutes. But they weren't surprised: theirs was the great hockey nation. It wasn't any different from what they were used to in the NHL.

And then things changed.

The Canadians seemed to get lost in the fog that was rising from the ice. At 11:40 of the first period, Soviet right wing Yevgeny Zimin opened up the Soviet scoring. That was okay, the Canadians thought. Dryden seemed a bit off balance. It was just one goal. The Canadians were still ahead.

The problem was, the Soviet goals kept coming.

Soviet player Vladimir Petrov scored just over 17 minutes into the first period. Valeri Kharlamov scored twice in the second.

Bobby took a slashing penalty around five minutes into the second. He was used to playing a rough and tough game. Would it work against the Soviets?

When Bobby got back out on the ice, it looked like the Canadians might be able to bounce back. While sitting to Tretiak's right, in perfect position, Bobby tapped in the puck that was passed to him by Ron Ellis. Goal! Bobby pumped his fist in triumph. He had scored his first goal in the most important hockey series in Canadian history. And it was an important goal. Did it mean that the Canadians would make their comeback? The crowd at the Forum slowly started to get louder.

But Bobby's goal would be the last one

for the Canadians that game.

The Soviets scored three more times. The final score of the first game in the series was 7–3.

It was a crushing defeat for Canada. The Summit Series was supposed to be a walk in the park. Reporters had called the series a victory for Canada before a single game was played. They laughed at the idea that the Canadians could be defeated by the Soviets. Columnists thought the idea of the Soviets winning even one game would be ridiculous.

But win it they did.

Many felt that it was just one bad game by the Canadians. Things seemed to look better for the Canadians after they won Game 2 with a score of 4–1.

Then Game 3 was a tie. Even though their team didn't lose, Canadian fans were upset that their boys weren't walking all over the Soviets.

By the time Game 4 came around, Canadian fans were starting to grumble. They started to get vocal. Boos echoed around the Pacific Coliseum, the Vancouver arena where the game was being played.

In the middle of the third period, the score was 4–2. Then, at 11:05, Soviet player Alexander Yakushev scored. Again the Canadians were on the losing end of a game. And they had won just one game. Their fans weren't impressed. Even a late goal from Dennis Hull couldn't help raise their spirits.

When the game was over, an emotional Phil Esposito took to the ice to be interviewed.

"For the people across Canada, we tried. We did our best. And for the people who boo us, geez, I'm really . . . all of us guys are really disheartened and disillusioned and we're disappointed in some of the people. And we can't believe the bad press we got, the booing we've gotten in our own arena . . ." he said, sweat dripping down his face. "I'm really, really disappointed. Some of our guys are really down in the dumps . . . They've got a really good team . . ."

Years later, Bobby had a different view of that game.

"You usually get what you deserve. And I think we deserved that [the boos]. We not only played a poor game in Vancouver, we were very undisciplined, very stupid. I think we deserved what we got from the fans."

Bobby wasn't one to give up. He knew how important the series was to the people of Canada. And it was hockey. It was what he lived to play. It was a matter of pride. So he and the other players became more determined than ever.

From that fourth game, things seemed to turn for the Canadians. After a break from the series, the team headed to Moscow. Many Canadian fans made the trip to support their team, even though they looked certain to lose.

In Game 5, Team Canada played the best two periods they'd had so far. They were up 3–0 midway through the second period. But then the Russians came on strong. Even though things looked good for the Canadians, and Bobby had two points, something went terribly wrong. In just 11 shots on goal, the Russians scored five goals. The Canadians lost again.

The Canadians went on to win Games 6 and 7. And the series was getting physical. Paul Henderson had suffered a concussion in the fifth game, but refused to listen to doctors. He continued to play. In Game 6, Bobby took to the ice against the Soviet line that included Valeri Kharlamov. Kharlamov had been an important player throughout the series for the Soviets.

Bobby Clarke skates around the net in the Summit Series. Bobby's performance on a line with Ron Ellis and Paul Henderson was a surprise for many.

When Kharlamov came up against Bobby, he got a two-handed slash on an already sore ankle. Bobby's slash broke the Soviet player's ankle, but Kharlamov finished the game.

Many Soviets thought the slash proved that Canadian players were nothing but thugs. Even Canadians were shocked by it. Many believed it was shameful. Bobby was highly criticized for it.

In an interview with hockey journalist Dick Beddoes, Bobby made no apology for his actions: "If I hadn't learned to lay on a two-hander once in a while, I'd never have left Flin Flon."

Over the years, there has been a lot of debate about that slash. Assistant coach John Ferguson was even blamed for telling Bobby to take Kharlamov out of the game. Bobby says that he doesn't remember being told to do it. Either way, it turned out to be something that Bobby has always been remembered for. It has followed him around ever since.

Going into Game 8, the series was tied. Bobby had five points. It was a must-win game for the Canadians. Even if it ended in a tie, the Soviets would claim to be the winners, as they'd scored more goals.

Either way, it was a game that would go down in history.

Heading into the third period, the Soviets were ahead 5–3. Then the Canadians came on strong. They scored within the first three minutes. Then scored again. The game was tied. The minutes were ticking away. It looked as though the series would end up tied, with the Soviets claiming victory. Then, with just over 30 seconds left in the game, came the most famous goal in Canadian history.

"Here's a shot. Henderson makes a wild stab for it and falls," famous broadcaster Foster Hewitt called. "Here's another shot. Right in front. They score!! Henderson has scored for Canada!"

Bobby had this to say when he reflected on the series years later: "I think we found that as the series progressed . . . it was a violent series, and there was a lot of harshness went on, but as our conditioning and our teamwork and stuff got better, we got better than them."

Summit Series '72 Stats

Game 1, Sept. 4	The Montreal Forum
	USSR 7 – Canada 3
Game 2, Sept. 5	Maple Leaf Gardens (Toronto)
	Canada 4 – USSR 1
Game 3, Sept. 6	Winnipeg Arena
	Canada 4 – USSR 4
Game 4, Sept. 8	Pacific Coliseum (Vancouver)
	USSR 5 – Canada 3
Game 5, Sept. 22	Luzhniki Ice Palace (Moscow, USSR)
	USSR 5 – Canada 4
Game 6, Sept. 24	Luzhniki Ice Palace
	Canada 3 – USSR 2
Game 7, Sept. 26	Luzhniki Ice Palace
	Canada 4 – USSR 3
Game 8, Sept. 28	Luzhniki Ice Palace
	Canada 6 – USSR 5

Canada wins the series 4–3–1 (4 wins, 3 losses, and 1 tie).

8 Bobby Clarke, Superstar

The Summit Series catapulted Bobby to hockey stardom. Even though his slash against Kharlamov bothered many, he had been an essential part of the Canadian victory. And he was the only player of the Summit Series to play in all eight games.

Bobby returned to the NHL a superstar. It was also clear that playing with the best in the league for such an important series had boosted his self-confidence.

In January 1973, at the age of twenty-three, Bobby was named captain of the Philadelphia Flyers. He was the youngest player to captain that team. Although Bobby considered himself quiet in the dressing room, he wasn't afraid to speak his mind — something he's still known for today. At the time, it was clear that Philadelphia management and coaches recognized how much he inspired the other young players on the team. That season, his third in the NHL, he scored 37 goals and 67 assists, for 104 points. It was his best season yet. He was on his way to becoming a Flyers legend.

Bobby became the first Flyers' player to win the Bill Masterton Trophy. This trophy goes to the NHL player who "best exemplifies the qualities of perseverance, sportsmanship, and dedication" to hockey. Bobby certainly persevered. And he certainly was dedicated.

Bobby also took home the Lester B.

Pearson Award that year. It means he was the most outstanding player in the NHL, as judged by the NHL Players' Association. He was also named to the Second All-Star team.

But on the ice, Bobby's team was becoming known as the Broad Street Bullies. (The arena in Philadelphia was on Broad Street.) The Flyers played rough. Bobby is famous for saying of their style of play: "We take the shortest route to the puck and arrive in ill humour."

Back then, it wasn't uncommon to see bench-clearing brawls. And you could be sure that Bobby would be in the middle of some shoving and pushing. The player who many had thought would be a possible weakness was showing how tough he really was.

And it wasn't just his physical presence on the ice that impressed fans. Bobby was still producing. In the 1973–74 season,

Bobby scored 35 goals and 52 assists, for 87 points. He also totalled 113 penalty minutes.

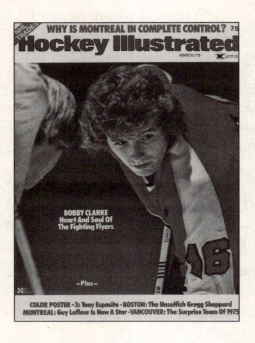

Bobby Clarke had risen to hockey stardom. He had become the face of the Flyers and represented a tough Philadelphia team that had come to be known for its grittiness.

But the Philadelphia Flyers were making a bad name for themselves throughout the league. Many thought that their style of play went beyond what was acceptable in hockey. Bobby had no problem with being part of that image. He was unapologetic for his rough play. Some felt that he was brash and arrogant.

When the Flyers made the Stanley Cup finals and faced the Boston Bruins, Bobby Clarke had one of his best moments.

It was Game 2 of the series, and the score was tied at 2–2. The players were tired. The Flyers had already lost the first game to Boston, and wanted a win before heading home to play in Philadelphia. So each one of them tried their hardest to put the puck in the net. But nobody tried as hard as Bobby.

And his hard work paid off.

At just over the 12-minute mark of sudden-death overtime, Flyers winger Bill

Flett passed the puck to Bobby, who was crossing just in front of the Boston net. Bobby fired a backhand shot at Boston goalie Gilles Gilbert. The puck rebounded. Bobby wasn't about to let that rebound sit. He took another shot, putting the puck right in the back of the net. His jump for joy is a moment that will live on in the hearts of many Flyers' fans.

The unlikely win sent Philadelphia back home. And there, they won the next two games. They lost the fifth game to Boston 5–1; a crushing defeat. But in Game 6 — a must-win game for Boston, a possible Stanley Cup victory for the Flyers — Philadelphia shut out Boston with a 1–0 victory.

The toothless smile on Bobby's face was enormous as he and Bernie Parent, the winner of the Conn Smythe Trophy as MVP for the championship, hoisted the Cup. They skated through the crowd of

reporters and photographers who lined
the ice. Bobby had won the ultimate prize,
the oldest and most coveted trophy in pro
sports. The small boy from Flin Flon had
reached his ultimate dream.

*Bobby clutches the Stanley Cup, the ultimate prize in
hockey. After a tough series, the Flyers came back to
win the 1973-74 Cup.*

Bobby followed up his Stanley Cup win with the best two seasons of his career. In 1974–75, he scored 27 goals and 89 assists, for 116 points. His penalty minutes also increased. The following season he scored 30 goals and 89 assists, for 119 points. Again, his penalty minutes went up. Bobby was playing the game both offensively and defensively.

Bobby continued to play a strong game. And he was a definite presence on the ice, a force to be reckoned with. He was accused of being a bully on the ice, but he didn't let it affect his game. He continued to post decent numbers, although 1975–76 was to be the best season of his career.

In all, Bobby Clarke won the Hart Memorial Trophy (MVP for the regular season) three times: 1972, 1975, and 1976. He won the Lester Patrick Trophy for outstanding service to hockey in the

United States in 1976, and the Frank J. Selke Award, which goes to a forward who excels in the defensive aspects of hockey, in 1980. He was also named to the First All-Star team twice (in 1975 and 1976) and to the Second All-Star team twice (in 1973 and 1974).

Bobby no longer had anything to prove. He was a proven scorer, a proven defensive player, a proven leader. Nowhere along the way had he let his diabetes come between him and the thing he loved most in his life — hockey.

Bobby had great seasons following his career-best 1975–76, but he decided to call an end to his days on the ice when he was still quite young. He retired in 1984 at the age of 35. Bobby had already decided that he wasn't leaving hockey behind. He became an assistant coach to the Flyers while still a player in 1979. He continued in that role right up until he announced his retirement in 1984, a sad day for many Flyers fans. Bobby was paid the ultimate hockey honour when he was inducted into Canada's Hockey Hall of Fame on June 15, 1987.

Bobby was never too far from Philadelphia. After his resignation, he was named Senior Vice President and General Manager of the Flyers. He stayed in that role for six years. He served as Senior Vice President for a year after that, and then went on to become the President and General Manager of the team. After nine seasons, he stepped down as President, but remained as General Manager. Today, he continues to serve as Senior Vice President to the team. Many nights, fans can find him at the arena, watching the new Flyers taking to the ice amid cheers — cheers that once greeted him as he stepped onto the ice.

In a Flyers tribute to Bobby Clarke, it

*Bobby Clarke (far left) as the Philadelphia Flyers'
general manager at the 1998 draft with Simon Gagne.*

was noted that he was fond of saying, "I
never thought I was working hard; it was
just the only way I knew how to play the
game."

Maybe so. And it was lucky for
Philadelphia fans that it was the only way
he knew how to play.

Bobby Clarke's Stats

(GP: Games Played; G: Goals; A: Assists;
P: Points)

YEAR	GP	G	A	P
1969–70	76	15	31	46
1970–71	77	27	36	63
1971–72	78	35	46	81
1972–73	78	37	67	104
1973–74	77	35	52	87
1974–75	80	27	89	116
1975–76	76	30	89	119
1976–77	80	27	63	90
1977–78	71	21	68	89
1978–79	80	16	57	73
1979–80	76	12	57	69
1980–81	80	19	46	65
1981–82	62	17	46	63
1982–83	80	23	62	85
1983–84	73	17	43	60

Epilogue

Bobby Clarke may have been one of the first famous Canadian sports stars to have diabetes, but many other famous Canadians — and athletes — also have it. Today, Nick Boynton of the Anaheim Ducks, Toby Petersen of the Dallas Stars, and Brandon Crombeen of the St. Louis Blues are just three NHL players who have it. But being diagnosed with diabetes thirty years ago was very different from being diagnosed today.

When Bobby was playing hockey, it was typical for someone like him to have to inject himself with a needle. Inside the needle would have been long-acting insulin, which would last for a large part of the day. If someone has low blood sugar, they can feel dizzy, be confused, and look pale. If a diabetic's blood sugar runs too low, he or she could even pass out. It is important, if a person ever does lose consciousness due to low blood sugar, that they get something sweet into their mouths. They can't drink anything, as they run the risk of choking. What is recommended is rubbing cake icing into their mouths.

One of the most incredible advancements for diabetics has been the insulin pump. This device was just a dream when Bobby was diagnosed. The pump is attached to a small tube that is injected into a diabetic's skin. Once attached, it delivers insulin to the person throughout the day. When someone using an insulin pump eats, he or she enters into the machine the amount of carbohydrates in the meal. The machine calculates the amount of fast-acting insulin needed. Once the person programs it, the machine delivers the insulin under the skin, right into the body.

Although Nick Boynton doesn't wear his pump during games, Toby Petersen wears his tucked into his hockey pants. Of course, in the punishing sport of hockey, the pump can take a beating. In one game, Petersen's pump took a hit from a puck. But it didn't stop him from wearing it. He just keeps needles as backup in case of damage to his pump.

Bobby Clarke was lucky enough to only ever have had one time where he experienced an extreme blood sugar low. Perhaps it is another testament to how tough he really was. He never wanted to be considered a "diabetic hockey player."

"When I turned pro, I said 'I'm a hockey player with diabetes.' If I played poorly, it was because I played poorly. If I played good, it was because I played good. Diabetes had nothing to do with it."

Glossary

AHL: The American Hockey League is a minor hockey league that was formed in 1940. Many professional hockey players start off in this league after being drafted by an NHL team.

Carbs: Carbohydrates are a major nutrient found in most foods. They are an important source of energy.

Cold War: A period of hostility from 1945 to 1991 between the United States, as well as its allies from World War II, and the Soviet Union.

(NHL Entry) Draft: A yearly event where rights to unsigned players are spread out among NHL teams.

Exhibition game: A game played before the official NHL season starts that doesn't count in the NHL standings.

Five-hole: The area between a goalie's leg pads.

Icing: A shot from a player's own side of centre ice that goes, without being touched, past the end red line of the other team's side. If this happens, there is a stop in play and another faceoff is taken from the shooting team's end.

Insulin: A hormone produced by the pancreas (a gland in the body) that helps control the sugar level in blood. Diabetics have to be given injections of insulin.

Killing a penalty: When a team is playing with fewer players on the ice (because one of their players is serving a penalty), and they still manage to prevent the other team from scoring, they are said to have "killed the penalty."

MVP: Most valuable player.

Penalty: A punishment given to a player for going against certain rules of the game. Minor penalties are two minutes; major penalties are five minutes.

Right wing: A forward position on a hockey team that plays to the right of the centre.

Roster: The list of players on a team.

Saves (n): The number of times a goalie prevents the puck from going into the net.

Shutout (n) or Shut out (v): A game where the goalie doesn't let in a goal; the act of.

Slot: The area right in front of a net.

Starter/Starting (as in starting goalie): The goalie who starts the game for a team.

Zone: One of the three sections on the ice: defensive zone (the area within a team's blueline); offensive zone (the area inside the defensive team's blueline); and the neutral zone (the area between the two bluelines marked on the ice).

Acknowledgements

I'd like to thank Bobby Clarke for taking the time to speak with me, and to Zack Hill and Brian Smith of the Philadelphia Flyers for all their help. Also, a very special thank you to Craig Campbell of the Hockey Hall of Fame and to Paul Romanuk.

Photo Credits

The Hockey Hall of Fame: p. 15, p. 20, p. 30, p. 47, p. 54, p. 67, p. 81
University of Toronto Image Bank: p. 35
The Philadelphia Flyers: p. 74

Author's Note

Bobby Clarke's story is one that means very much to me. When my daughter was diagnosed with Type 1 Diabetes two days after her fourth birthday, I was shocked. I was even a little scared. My father had had Type 2 Diabetes, so I knew about that. But shots? Every day? How would she cope?

Then, I remembered Bobby Clarke.

He was a tough guy. That's how I remembered him. I had forgotten that he'd had diabetes. So, if I had forgotten that, did it really matter that my own daughter had it?

Of course it did. It wasn't something that I could ignore. But Bobby's story *did* remind me that diabetes didn't have to hold her back. She could still go on living her life. She could still do whatever it was she put her mind to.

Diabetes is something you can manage.

Someone who has been diagnosed with it might be scared, shocked, and angry. My daughter was. So were her father and I. But I've come to see that she can still live the life she wants. Nothing has to stop her. And now, especially, there are so many advancements in the world of diabetes. Already an artificial pancreas is being tested. This device would monitor a diabetic patient's blood sugar while supplying the proper insulin every minute.

I often think of Bobby's toothless grin. Did that look like someone who was letting a disease hold him back?

It might have been easier for Bobby to feel sorry for himself. It might have been easier for him to give up on his dream. But, even at thirteen years old, Bobby showed how much of a fighter he really was. Nothing was going to hold him back.

"Diabetes never affected the way I played hockey," he says.

He encourages others to hold fast to their dreams. "You can't use diabetes as an excuse . . . you need to learn to take care of yourself.

"Diabetes can't control your life," he said. "You have to control *it*."

Index